Jed's Junior Space Patrol

HELP!

Spaceship Ace landed on Planet X5.
Jed's parents
got ready to leave the ship.
They were cargo pilots.
Today they were picking up
spare parts for rockets.

“Can I go with you?” asked Jed.
“No,” said his mother.
“We won’t be gone long.”
Jed was mad.
“You always say that,” he said.
His parents waved good-bye and left.
Jed took out a computer game,
but he didn’t feel like playing.

"Help!"

Who said that?

Jed looked around the spaceship.

No one was there.

"Help!"

The cry was coming from outside.

It was pulling him like a rope.

Jed peeked out the door.

He didn't see his parents.

Jed started running.

He ran and ran

until he came to a cave.

"Help!"

The cry was louder.

Slowly Jed went in.

He saw a strange animal
lying under a rock.
He could tell it was hurt.

"Help!" said the animal.

"I'm trapped."

It talked

without moving its mouth.

Jed tried to push the rock away,

but it was too heavy.

“Please,” said the animal.
“Take care of my babies.”
The animal died
before it could say more.
Jed saw two small animals
hiding behind their mother.

Would they bite?

Jed held out a hand.

One of the animals licked it.

The other said "Thank you"

in a high squeaky voice.

Like its mother, it talked

without moving its mouth.

Jed put the animals

inside his spacesuit.

Then he ran back to Spaceship Ace.

His parents were waiting.

"Where did you go?" they asked.

They had been very worried.

Jed showed them the animals

and told them what happened.

Suddenly the door buzzed.

It was a Planet X5 patrolman.

"I see you found your boy," he said.

Then he saw the animals.

"Where did you find cogs?" he asked.

"Find what?" asked Jed.

"Cogs," said the patrolman.
"They are called cogs
because they look a little like cats
and a little like dogs.

I must take them to Headquarters.
Give them to me."

"No, no!" the cogs said.

Jed held them tight.

"They want to stay with me," he said.

"Sorry," said the patrolman.

"Cogs are very rare,

and they have special powers.

Commander May wants to find out

what their powers are."

"But their mother told me

to take care of them," said Jed.

"Don't be silly," said the patrolman.

"Cogs can't talk."

He took the cogs and left.

TEDDY TO THE RESCUE

Jed's father looked mad.

"Were you lying about the cogs?"

he asked.

"No," said Jed.

"The cogs really can talk to me."

But Jed's father didn't believe him.

Jed felt awful.

Everyone was mad,

and the cogs were gone.

Suddenly he heard one talk.

"We are at Headquarters," it said.

Jed jumped up.

"Did you hear that?" he asked.

"Hear what?" his father said.

Jed sat down.

Only he could hear the cogs.

When they talked,

they did not move their mouths.

Maybe he could do the same thing.

"Hi," he thought.

"Hi," they said.

"Can you hear me?" he thought.

"Yes," they said.

"Where are you?" he thought.

"In a big blue cage," they said.

Jed jumped up again.

"Maybe we can get the cogs back,"

he said out loud to his mother.

"Forget the cogs," she said.

She showed Jed a big box.

"Here," she said.
"We got you this today
so you won't be lonely anymore."
Jed opened the box.

Inside was a big teddy bear
with wheels on its feet.
"A teddy bear?" yelled Jed.
"I'm eight years old!"
"It's not an ordinary bear,"
said his mother.
"It's a teddy robot computer.
It's programmed to take care of you
and to be your friend."
But Jed didn't want
a teddy robot computer.
He wanted his cogs.

“Now you may go out, Jed,”
said his father.

"Your robot will watch you.
Be back at two thirty for takeoff."
Jed ran down the ramp.
The bear skated after him.
Jed ran as fast as he could,
but the bear skated faster.
Dumb robot, thought Jed.
He stuck his foot out.
Teddy fell.

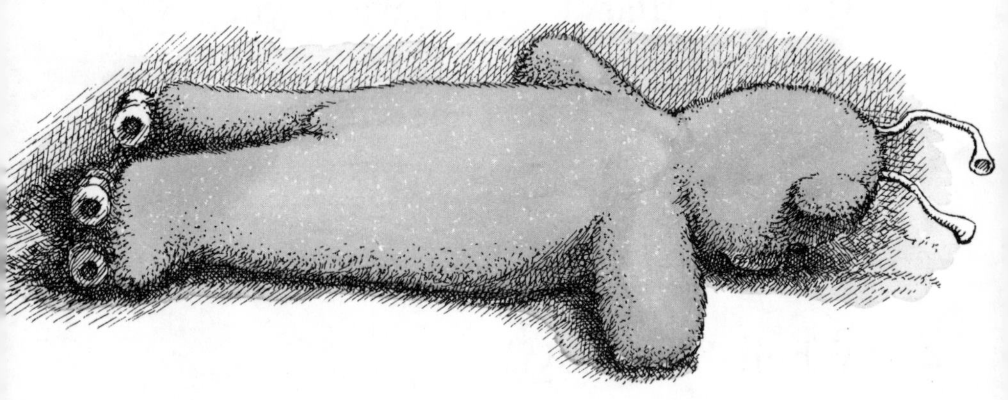

"Why are you so mean?"

the bear asked.

"I'm sorry," said Jed.

"It's just that I don't want you.

I want my cogs.

I have to take care of them."

"Why didn't you say so?" asked Teddy.

"Where are they?"

"In a big blue cage at Headquarters. That's all I know," said Jed.

Dit-dit-dit-dit-ding!

A paper came out of Teddy's nose.

It said, "The big blue cage
is in Room 31.
Go in the side door.
Take Ramp 3."
Jed was amazed.
"Come on," said Teddy.
"Let's go!"

A SECRET PLACE

Jed and Teddy raced to Headquarters
as fast as they could.
They went in the side door.
They took Ramp 3 to Room 31.
"Oh, no!
It's locked!" said Jed.

"Relax," said Teddy.

He put his paw on the lock.

Click. Click.

The door opened.

"How did you do that?" asked Jed.

"Easy," said Teddy.

"I have a computer inside me."

Jed saw the cage and the cogs.

"Here we are!" they said.

Jed lifted the cogs out of the cage.

"Where can I hide them?" he asked.

"No sweat," said Teddy.

Click. Click.

A secret door opened in his chest.

"Great!" said Jed.

At two thirty
they were back at Spaceship Ace.
"I see you and your bear are pals,"
said Jed's father.
"That's right," said Jed.
"Don't think about the cogs,"
said his mother.
"I'm sure they are safe."
"They sure are," said Jed.
As Spaceship Ace blasted off,
Jed hugged Teddy.
Inside Teddy's warm, fuzzy coat
was a computer and a secret place.

Inside the secret place
were the cogs.
"Don't worry," Jed thought.
"We won't," they said.
"As long as we're with you."

FIRE COMING!

The next day Commander May's ship pulled up next to Spaceship Ace. The two ships hooked together. Then Commander May came aboard. "Do you have the cogs?" she asked. "No," said Jed's parents.

Jed did not say a word.

"They escaped," said Commander May.

"We must find them.

Men, search the ship."

Her patrolmen searched everywhere.
Jed heard the cogs crying.
He put his arm around Teddy
and felt the cogs shaking inside.
"Don't worry," he thought.
"The patrolmen won't find you."
"We know that," they said.
"But something else is wrong.

We can feel it!"

"What is it?" thought Jed.

"We don't know," said the cogs.

"But it is coming close,

and it is very hot!"

Jed was scared.

He didn't know what to do.

The cogs started yelling,
"Fire coming! Turn!"
Jed was too afraid to talk.
"FIRE COMING! TURN!"
screamed the cogs.
Only Jed could hear them.
He had to do something!
At last he yelled,
"FIRE COMING! TURN!"
"What?" asked the commander.
Everyone looked confused.
Suddenly
Teddy skated to the controls.
He put a paw on a dial.

Zoom!

The spaceship turned so fast
that everyone fell down.

Swish!

A ball of fire flew by the window.
The spaceship got so hot,
Jed thought he would burn up.

At last the air cooled.

"That was a giant starburst,"

said Jed's mother.

"Yes," said Commander May.

"It almost crashed into us.

Your son and his bear

saved our lives."

THE POWER OF THE COGS

"Jed," said the commander,
"how did you know
the starburst was coming?"
Jed was afraid to tell,
but he knew he had to.
"Show them, Teddy," he said.

Teddy popped open his secret door.

"The cogs!" said the commander.

"How did they get here?"

Jed held the cogs in his arms.

"They speak to me," he said.

"They told me that fire was coming."

"I see," said the commander.
"So that is their special power.
They can sense danger,
and they can send thought waves."
Commander May took the cogs.
She tried to be nice to them,
but they growled at her.

"They don't want to go with you,"
said Jed.
"They need to stay with me
because I understand them."

Commander May gave the cogs back.
"You're right," she said.
"Those cogs belong with you.
But I may need them someday.
If I do, will you
bring them to me?"
Jed smiled.
"If my parents let me," he said.
Commander May told Jed's parents
she would take good care of him.
"Jed and Teddy and the cogs
are a great team," she said.

"I think they should have a name."

Dit-dit-dit-dit-ding!

A paper came out of Teddy's nose.

"Jed's Junior Space Patrol,"
it said.
"That's perfect!" said the commander.
And everyone agreed.

Jed's Junior Space Patrol

A Science Fiction Easy-to-Read

Jean and Claudio Marzollo
pictures by David S. Rose

DIAL BOOKS FOR YOUNG READERS
NEW YORK

For Nonna and Nonno
J.M. and C.M.

For Arthur
D.S.R.

This special edition for Education Reading Services, Inc.
is published by arrangement with
Dial Books for Young Readers
A Division of E. P. Dutton
A Division of New American Library
2 Park Avenue
New York, New York 10016

Library of Congress Cataloging in Publication Data
Marzollo, Jean. Jed's Junior Space Patrol.
Summary: Jed, his Teddy bear robot, and two
creatures called cogs save Spaceship Ace.
[1. Science fiction] I. Marzollo, Claudio. II. Title.
PZ7.M3688Je [E] 81-12483 AACR2
ISBN 0-8037-4288-6
ISBN 0-8037-4287-8 (lib. bdg.)

The art for each picture consists of a black line-drawing
with two overlays prepared in wash and reproduced
in blue and orange halftone.

Reading Level 1.9